GRAYBOY

KAY CHORAO

HENRY HOLT AND COMPANY

NEW YORK

Henry Holt and Company, LLC
Publishers since 1866
115 West 18th Street
New York, New York 10011

Henry Holt is a registered trademark of Henry Holt and Company, LLC
Copyright © 2002 by Kay Sproat Chorao
All rights reserved.
Distributed in Canada by H. B. Fenn and Company Ltd.

Library of Congress Cataloging-in-Publication Data
Chorao, Kay.
Grayboy / Kay Chorao
Summary: A girl, her friend Robert, and her grandparents spend a summer enjoying
nature and the creatures that live in an East Coast bay, especially
one wounded seagull they name Grayboy.
[1. Gulls—Fiction. 2. Beaches—Fiction. 3. Ecology—Fiction.] I. Title.
PZ7.C4463 Gr 2002 [Fic]—dc21 2001000698

ISBN 0-8050-6411-7 / First Edition—2002 / Designed by Martha Rago
The artist used gouache on watercolor paper to create the illustrations for this book.
Printed in the United States of America on acid-free paper. ∞
1 3 5 7 9 10 8 6 4 2

This book is dedicated with love to Betty Wojciechowski,
who spent so many summers from childhood until the very end
enjoying Peconic Bay and all its wildlife,
and who now guards its waters.

It is almost summer. The bay is calm, just brushed in the middle by an offshore wind. A family of swans glides by. Seagulls squawk and circle above the water. All but one gray.

He quietly hops along the beach.

"Hello, bird," I say.

Frightened, the seagull flaps away on one wing. He hops onto a rock and watches me.

I stand in the water watching back, but the water laps icy cold on my feet and I look down. Minnows nibble my toes and it tickles.

"Ha, ha," I laugh.

The minnows scatter, flashing bits of silver. They are called shiners, and Robert uses them for bait. Robert is my best friend.

When I look back, the seagull is gone.

One day while Grandma and I are collecting shells, we see the seagull again. He watches us from a distance, perched on a buoy.

"Hello, bird," I yell.

He flaps his wing and sails crookedly into the water.

Gram and I collect all kinds of shells: slipper snails, scallops, mussels, oysters, razor clams, moonsnails, tiny ceriths, and jingle shells, my favorites. Sometimes we find starfish, dried by the sun, but not today. The shells will go in a special box. On rainy days we will open the box and make shell jewelry. Even Robert.

As Gram and I walk along the beach, the gray seagull bobs along, just offshore.

When I toss him a slipper snail, he swims in and pecks out the meat.

Gram and I laugh, and throw him more.

As the water warms, Robert and I swim almost every day. We wait for high tide, when the jetty rocks are covered with water.

Robert calls Grandma "spacewoman" because she wears goggles.

Grandma swims laps, and Robert and I play dolphin. We dive into the water and pop out again. Sometimes Robert splashes me and I splash back. Sometimes we catch jellyfish. They glimmer in our hands.

Grandma says, "No throwing jellies."

We giggle and throw after she looks away.

Grandma teaches us to kick from the hips and breathe, and when we grow tired and shivery, she says, "All out for a hot shower."

When we scramble out of the water, the gray gull hops away.

"He doesn't fly?" asks Robert.

"A hurt wing," I say.

Grandpa tosses him a crust of bread.

Other gulls swarm, seeming to appear from nowhere. A big white herring gull swoops down and grabs the bread.

"Poor fellow," says Grandpa.

He tosses another bread scrap. This time our gull gobbles it down.

Robert finds a crab, and our gull pecks out the meat, even while the other gulls wheel and shriek.

We name our gull Grayboy.

Every day we look for Grayboy on the beach.

He gets to know us and hops over when we bring bread or minnows.

The other seagulls circle and dive into the bay. They catch crabs, which they drop on the rocks to crack. Sometimes one gull swoops down and steals a crab. Then all the others chase the thief.

Grayboy can only watch.

So Robert and I go crab hunting for him.

We head for the point. That is where the land juts into the bay. An inlet with marsh grass runs along one edge. The crabs scuttle along offshore. They hide in the sand and wave their claws.

Robert catches a rock crab, while I explore the shore. I find rows of little holes in the sand. I crouch and wait for a face to poke out. Instead, quick as a flash, a little fiddler crab pops in. I dig and dig, but I can't find him. But another pops out of his hole and I grab him.

All along the shore little mole crabs rise from the sand with passing waves, then disappear. Hermit crabs skitter along the shallows, looking like snails. They are my favorites. I pick one up and watch it curl deep into the mollusk shell, its borrowed home. As hermits grow, they find larger and larger shells to carry on their backs and hide in.

All summer long we find crabs for Grayboy or net minnows for him.

We swim near him while he bobs on the waves.

We build sand castles for him to perch on, moats for him to wade in, and when we see children throwing rocks at him we chase them away and yell bad words as loud as we can.

Grandma says, "Hush, children! Where did you learn that language?" But she strides up the beach and has words with their parents.

We love Grayboy. He cocks his head in a comic way. It makes us laugh. He hops to greet us and throws back his head to make seagull squawks when we leave.

"Don't worry," we tell him. "We will see you tomorrow."

Early one morning Robert goes fishing with his father. I hear the motor and see the boat headed east.

"Storm's coming," Grandpa says at breakfast.

Clouds blot out the sun, except for an eerie pink glow. Whitecaps dot the bay. Waves slap the shore.

Grandpa takes me to the deli on the back of his bike to buy a newspaper. I burrow my nose in Grandpa's shirt. It smells of fresh air from hanging on Grandma's clothesline.

"Hold on tight," says Grandpa.

At a little bridge we pass a family of swans.

"Stay with your parents, little ones. Storm's coming," Grandpa calls.

Coming back home we see a muskrat, scuttling through the tall grass.

"Hurry home, George. Storm's coming," calls Grandpa.

When we get home, Grandma is struggling to pull the sailboat away from the pounding surf. Grandpa and I come to help.

"We'll lock her in the boathouse," Grandpa yells. The wind blows his words away, but Grandma nods, and we pull and push the boat into the boathouse.

Nearby is a bucket of shiners. I know Robert must have left them.

"Breakfast for Grayboy," I say.

Gram and Gramp can't hear. They are heading up the steps, home, and the wind is taking my words.

So I half bury the bucket next to the boathouse, where Grayboy will be able to find it. Then I hurry up the steps after them.

All along the bay, boats strain at their moorings and thrash violently. The wind is picking up.

Rain breaks from the sky and pounds our windows.

The wind slams our shutters. BANG, BANG, BANG! The whole house seems to rock. I am scared. I want Robert to be there, too. But then I remember.

"Robert is out fishing, Gram!" I cry.

"Surely not," Grandpa says.

He finds his binoculars and scans the bay. Everything is blurry with rain, the waves wild, driven by the wind.

A boat has broken its moorings down-beach and is crashing against a bulkhead. Some men are trying to rescue it, but the waves knock them over. The tide is too high.

Gram is on the telephone with Robert's mother.

"Oh dear, I'm so sorry. Phone if there is any word, or if I can help."

My heart races.

Robert is out there.

My eyes fill with tears.

Robert.

Grandma rocks me in the old rocker, the way she did when I was little. She says, "There, there, don't fret. He'll be fine." But her face looks worried.

Grandpa paces. Then he goes to the kitchen and makes scrambled eggs and buttered toast.

I can't eat.

I try to play Chinese checkers with Grandma, but I can't think.

Grandpa reads to me, but I don't hear the words.

Robert, I think. *Robert.*

When the telephone rings, I know it is Robert's mother.

"Yes, Nancy, yes," says Grandma. "Well, thank heavens, thank heavens."

"He's alive! He's alive!" I yell, hopping up and down.

Grandma hangs up the phone.

"You see? I told you he would be fine. Just a little scraped and bruised. They had engine problems, and the boat got pushed up on the rocks."

The next day is bright and clear. Robert arrives early to show me his bandages. He is proud of them.

"Now you are injured, just like Grayboy," I say.

We race to the beach to find him.

We look up and down.

Overhead, seagulls soar and dive into the bay and shriek. But no Grayboy.

By the boathouse I find the bucket Robert left. The minnows are gone. Where the dunes rise behind the boathouse we find something gray, half buried in the sand.

We drop to our knees. Grayboy. "Oh, no," we cry. "Grayboy."

Robert lifts him into the bucket, and we carry him to the point. I dig a hole above the high-tide line, and we bury him.

"He was a good gull," I say.

"Brave," says Robert.

"I will miss him," I say.

"Me, too," says Robert.

"Gramp said he would never make it through the winter," I say.

"I know," says Robert.

We would like to cry, but we do not. We gave Grayboy a happy summer, but he gave us one, too.

"Good-bye, Grayboy," says Robert.

"Good-bye, Grayboy," I say.

On the bay the swan family glides by. Soon the cygnets will grow as large as the parents. Somewhere out on the water a loon cries, and a V formation of Canada geese skim the surface. They are migrating south for the winter.

I grab Robert's hand and we run. We pound barefoot along the beach, scrubbed clean by the storm. We leave footprints, side by side. Soon the tide will wash them away. But we will make countless more, and we will never forget our summer with Grayboy.

AUTHOR'S NOTE

This book was written to celebrate the wonder and beauty of Peconic Bay, Long Island, New York. The details are based on direct observation over many summers, and there really was a Grayboy, whom we fed and tried to protect one summer.

Like other bays and estuaries along the eastern coast of the United States, the ecology of Peconic Bay is fragile. Even since the book was begun, the horseshoe crabs, once ubiquitous, have grown scarcer. Piping plovers, who once filled the air, are almost extinct. And so it is hoped that we can learn to respect and protect this very special place and all the others like it so that they exist for future generations.